Table of Contents

Scrub

Chapter 1: Flight

She was a beautiful doe, heavy with fawn; but her graceful, sinewy legs trembled on the verge of collapse in the belly-deep expanse of maddening whiteness. Snow - sparkling, cold, cruel, endless - clutched at her exhausted body. Mile after weary mile she had plunged on - confident at first in her supple strength, now desperate, barely able to lift her sagging body in short stumbling hops.

She had paused for a brief moment in the open field, but this was no time to rest. Within seconds, the cedar swamp she had just left disgorged two yapping, howling hound dogs. They bounded lightly over the glistening snow - the same snow that had so lately engulfed the slender legs of the doe.

Catching sight of each other, the hunted and hunters once more redoubled their efforts. With a series of desperate plunges, the doe struggled to the edge of the field and onto a hard-packed and well-traveled road. Suddenly, the shackles dropped from her legs. Her bounds lengthened as she pulled away from the straining dogs.

Her good fortune was not to last, however. For the road led past a house, and the smell of man. In this case, the man would gladly have sheltered the wretched doe. But she couldn't have known that. Her instinct told her to shun the man. With one surging leap she cleared the fence at the side of the road and sank once more into the snowy depths.

The race could not go on. It might last another mile, or two at best. But the doe was sure to wear out. She made the first mile, then spent a large share of her last reserves on the second. As she slowed again, the smaller dog swung out to the right and circled to face his prey. Another hundred yards and the once proud doe stood at bay with one dog snapping at her heels, the other at her nose.

But there is no surrender in nature's children. They cherish life to the last struggling breath - and this doe was no exception. If the dogs had pushed her for another mile she might have dropped limp and helpless to the ground. But they stopped her too soon. Reaching down into her inner reserves and beyond, the doe raised her head for this - her final stand.

Rearing defiantly, she struck with surprising force, catching the dogs by surprise with her flint-like hooves. Having won the chase, the dogs had expected an easy victory. Instead, they found themselves yelping in pain as the doe's well-aimed kicks struck home.

Wary now, the dogs circled the doe - looking for a weak spot. Sensing their fear, she pawed at her attackers. Her angry hooves grazed a jaw, thumped a belly, and threatening more damage, she charged again and again. Although the dogs had reveled in

4

the chase, they had no real lust for fight. Being little more than domestic wolves, they saw no sport in cracked ribs and skulls - especially if they were their own.

Moments before they had been closing in for the kill. Now, tails tucked between their legs, they looked more like a humbled pair of hound dogs.

Suddenly they remembered - there would be milk in a pan and safety back at the barn. And so, with a final bark and a yowl, they turned tail and disappeared over the nearest hill.

With her tormentors finally gone, the doe relaxed for the first time in many hours. She sank exhausted into the snowy blanket of cool, refreshing, and restful white. For two full days the doe rested where the chase had ended, eating snow to quench her thirst. But instinct, and stirrings within her body, told her that she must move on. She must find food, and a secluded retreat safe from snooping dogs or prowling coyotes.

It was lack of good eating in an over-grazed deer-yard that had forced her to leave the protection of the herd. Then a farmer's haystack had tempted her into an open field, leading to the near-fatal chase. Fortunately, the humbled hound dogs were young and inexperienced at running deer. Otherwise, the doe would not have lived to profit by her experience.

Now she moved slowly, cautiously, but steadily downhill. It was early evening and the long northern twilight would give her plenty of time to reach a suitable cedar thicket in the dense recesses of a swamp.

She must find a safe place, a secluded place. If she did not choose wisely now, there would not be a second chance.

True, the snow was too deep, the season too early for a helpless fawn to be dropped into an icy world. The woods would be gripped in the icy fingertips of winter for at least another month - but that didn't matter at this moment. Her time had come.

She did choose well. Low hanging cedar and sprawling juniper would provide ample food while a mile or more of swamp spruce and balsam shut out the freezing wind from all directions. Early dawn found the doe nuzzling and nursing not one, but two delicately spotted fawns.

Chapter 2: Odds Against Them

It was a cold world the tiny creatures faced on the first day of their out-of-the-womb existence. The largest of the two, a female, was rather small. But her even smaller brother was a "scrub" if ever there was one.

It seemed impossible that these helpless, out-of-season babies of the woods could survive long in the face of the odds against them.

As is the case with so many of nature's children, their one source of hope was their mother. She alone must feed them, fear for them, guard them, fight for them. She too must wean them, teach them what to fear and what to trust, and finally thrust them out on their own to shift for themselves. Provided, of course, they lived that long.

The first and most persistent enemy threatening little Scrub and his sister was the ever-present cold. But the faithful doe was equal to that danger. For the first few days she cradled the fawns against her own body almost constantly. The thick, low-hanging cedar browse that surrounded her retreat provided food for her. She was able to eat without leaving the twins during those first few critical days when they were gaining a reserve of strength and body fat. This would protect them later on when their mother would find it necessary to leave in search of food for herself.

Occasionally the distant barking of a farm dog or the lonesome howl of a coyote caused the doe to stir uneasily in her hidden snow hollow. But as long as she refused to move, there would be no tell-tale tracks or scent to attract her enemies.

It was not many days until the bodies of the little fawns had melted the snow beneath them. They now rested on a bed of dry twigs and needles. By this time, Mother Deer was feeling the need of exercise and more food. She had stripped the cedar branches surrounding her little family as far as she could reach in all directions, as well as overhead.

For a few hours each day the welcome rays of the sun filtered down through the close-cropped bushes of the cedar hide-out. During this time the doe ventured out, each day a little farther, to satisfy her growing appetite. This was not for herself only. She must provide life-giving milk to her young. For a while, the doe had no trouble finding plenty of food, although she had to forage further each day to get it. This meant increasing danger to the fawns and herself as well.

As the days lengthened, the less shaded snow began to melt under the warmth of the sun. During the night, however, the soft wet snow on the surface would re-freeze. The resulting crust was not strong enough to support the sharp hooves of Mother

Deer. It did, however, offer ideal footing for hungry coyotes and increased their hunting range by many miles.

One moonlit night the doe lay curled about her fawns to shield them from the frosty air. Suddenly, she was startled from her half-sleep by the sound of padded feet on the frozen snow. There were no warning barks - just the soft footsteps of a lean coyote who also had young to feed. The padding feet bypassed Mother Deer's cedar clump, then suddenly stopped. There were telltale tracks there, and a scent - left by the hungry doe. She had foraged among willow shoots at the edge of a marshy spot, and it had not gone unnoticed.

Again the doe heard the padding feet approaching, and she knew her secret was out. She leaped to her feet with a sudden snort - but not to flee. She would fight for her helpless little ones. Her startled enemy faded into the nearest thicket to regroup.

Although he was young, the coyote was both shrewd and experienced. He knew there was nothing to be gained by attacking a full-grown deer. One hoof scar had been enough to last him a lifetime. But there were other ways for a patient hunter to get his meat. A doe that snorted and refused to run could mean only one thing - fawns.

The enemy pointed his nose to the sky and howled. It was a high-pitched, broken call that sent a shiver through the fearful doe. It also brought an answer from the coyote's hungry mate. The siege was on. From now on the fawns would not be safe even for a minute without their mother's presence, until the snow was gone and they could be moved to another place.

The silence was not broken again that night. Twice, however, the watchful mother scented the coyotes as they circled, checking her exact location.

As the sun rose the next morning, black-capped chickadees hopped about as usual while little Scrub and his sister nursed with their usual greed. But Mother Deer was plainly nervous. Instead of going in search of new feeding grounds she stamped about nervously, making close circles around her fawns. Here and there she nibbled a twig she had not quite cleaned before, or had rejected as being too old and tough.

However, as the day wore on Mother Deer saw no sign of ever present danger. Driven by her ravenous hunger, she finally ventured away from the hollow beneath the now ragged cedar clump. A slight breeze stirred through the swamp, as the watchful doe took pains to eat on the downwind side of her little family.

Mother Deer had snatched only a few desperate mouthfuls when her nose once again caught the dread scent of her enemy. Snorting angrily, she bounded back to her hollow. A coyote's gray form slunk into a cedar thicket where food for the hungry doe hung in abundance. But it might as well have been miles away, for Mother Deer dared not leave her fawns long enough to go after it.

The sly coyotes did not have to stay on guard 24 hours a day to accomplish their purpose. They took turns and showed themselves only once or twice a day, keeping the doe in a state of nervous fear day and night. The constant agitation as well as dwindling food supply caused the doe's milk supply to dwindle rapidly. It seemed the fawns were constantly trying to nurse. And both mother and offspring began to feel the cold more keenly.

A well-beaten path began to form between the snow hollow and the nearest food supply, as the result of Mother Deer's many quick rushes back and forth to snatch a few bits of food. One day as Mother Deer interrupted his eager nursing to make a dash for food, little Scrub impatiently scrambled over the edge of the hollow and trotted along the path in pursuit of his dinner. Close at his heels followed big sister.

At the end of the path they nursed, while Mother Deer ate her fill for the first time in over a week. Scrub's determination to get his dinner had saved the little family from starvation.

11

Scrub

Chapter 3:
Dangers - Seen and Invisible

With the coming of spring and the normal fawning season, Scrub and his sister were ready to follow Mother Deer in search of food. Although at the age of two months the twins were eating grass with their mother, they did not have the size and weight that usually goes with that age. Their mother, in the snow-bound cedar swamp, had not been able to provide them with the abundance of milk that most fawns enjoy. After all, most mothers are feeding on lush spring grass.

So, at the time of year when the average fawn is hidden away in the brush, the twins foraged with their mother morning and evening. They often frequented the edge of a farmer's grain and hay fields.

One morning the threesome approached a favorite rye field in the early gray light of dawn. Before stepping out of the woods, the cautious doe stopped to listen and sniff the breeze. Suddenly she raised her head. Her white flag flicked and she bounded eagerly out into the open field. Scrub and his twin likewise flicked their little white flags and bounded after their mother. There, enjoying the farmer's fine

13

stand of green rye, stood several yearling deer with an elderly, barren doe as leader and guardian.

One young buck seemed especially pleased to see Mother Deer. He proved to be Scrub's older brother, born the season before. Mother Deer rubbed noses with him, but stamped her foot in warning when he nudged between her and the twins.

When the sun came up the deer herd moved back into the protection of the woods. Old grandma doe led the way, and Mother Deer followed with the twins. The old one's experience would lessen the burden of watching for danger.

During the days the deer moved but little. They nibbled an occasional mushroom, or sampled the leaves on "popple" and basswood sprouts. Of course, Scrub had to sample everything his mother ate. But the young deer soon concluded that leeks and mushrooms were a pretty poor substitute for mother's milk.

Most of the leaves were far above Scrub's hungry little nose. The rye suited him just fine, but it seemed his mother never took him there except near early dawn or the dusk of evening.

Although the times of extreme hunger ended with the winter, danger in one form or another knows no season. It was a foggy morning late in May when Scrub was introduced to a type of danger that his instinct was not yet equipped to cope with.

Under cover of the protective fog the band of deer, still lead by the old wise one, had stayed much longer than usual in the rye field. Then, traveling down wind so their noses could warn them of any trailing enemies, they struck out cross country to explore new pastures.

The deer were nearing a familiar woodlot when suddenly the roar of a school bus engine broke over a sharp rise in the near-by road. The old leader stopped, freezing to statue-like stillness. Little Scrub and his sister crowded close to Mother Deer as she too stood motionless in the fog.

The yearlings hesitated for a moment. Then fearing the huge monster would try to head them off from the woodlot, they bolted past the old doe and made a dash for the only safety they knew. As their bouncing flags disappeared into the fog, the roaring of the engines was replaced by an even more terrifying squeal of brakes. Scrub heard a solid thud and a muffled bleat of pain. Then the strange creature roared on down the road.

Mother Deer sprang ahead of the wise one. There at the side of the road lay Scrub's older brother. He had not heeded the old leader's snort, and Scrub never saw him again. Scrub did realize, however, that there was danger connected with the roaring giants that traveled the wide straight paths.

Not many days after the tragic school bus encounter, the deer arrived at the rye field one

15

evening only to find the earth all soft and crumbly. Here and there a wisp of green barely stuck out above the freshly plowed field.

Impatiently Scrub followed his mother and the others as they wandered about the field nibbling a leaf here and there. Before long the old leader tired of such slim picking and struck out resolutely across the open field. That night Scrub had a late supper of quack grass. The herd ate by the light of the moon in an old abandoned apple orchard. For many days the band of deer came morning and evening to feed under the apple trees.

Scrub grazed and foraged right along with the older deer. He ate or at least sampled everything he saw his mother eat. But to his mind, there was still nothing quite equal to Mother Deer's milk. But the doe was beginning to show signs of impatience whenever the twins nudged her flanks. Gradually but surely she was withdrawing this luxury from her fawns. Not infrequently Scrub reached for a snack, only to be met by a well-aimed kick towards the end of his hungry nose.

Mother Deer's body had suffered a severe drain during her ordeal in the cedar swamp early that spring. The burden of feeding the twins on winter forage had worn her down. Now that the fawns could feed themselves, the doe wisely went about the business of replenishing her own reserves.

16

In spite of the ample supply of grass and the ideal location of the orchard, the deer herd eventually grew tired of quack grass. Their natural instinct offered protection from an unbalanced diet. Mother Deer especially never seemed able to satisfy her appetite, even though her stomach was filled to capacity most of the time.

It was mid-summer before Scrub and his family again followed the old leader back to the field where they had once enjoyed the farmer's rye. To their delight, the field was once more clothed in green. The ever-hungry Scrub did not find the half-grown potato plants as rewarding as the rye had been. But Mother Deer seemed to think they were wonderful.

Scrub finally decided that the strange-tasting potato leaves were better than an empty stomach. As he nibbled here and there, he soon learned that the new growth in the center of each plant was really quite satisfying.

One day, the little band had not yet finished their early morning feeding when they heard the put-put of a tractor at the far side of the field. Instantly, each animal was transformed into a living statue. As each deer eyed the noisy intruder, it began a steady, unhurried advance across one edge of the potato field. Behind the tractor followed another machine, whining constantly and belching forth great white clods on either side.

The old wise one regarded this invasion without undue alarm. Farm machines were nothing new to her. But she did know the price of carelessness. It seems that even farmers sometimes develop an appetite for venison. So she remained motionless until the machines made one complete trip across the field and started back again. Then, satisfied that her charges were in no danger, the old doe resumed her feeding.

Once when the tractor slowed to make a turn at the end of a row, the motor backfired. Scrub had never seen such a waving of white flags as the herd disappeared into the brush at the edge of the woods. Following the example of their mother, Scrub and his sister were soon relaxing with her in the seclusion of a basswood thicket.

Each day there was something new for the twins to learn - something that could not be provided for by an inherited instinct. For Scrub's ancestors had lived for centuries unmolested by noisy motors, and had never feasted on rye and potatoes.

By mid-morning, the noise in the potato field had died away. That evening the little herd was back again with fresh appetites. As Scrub looked out of the bushes and over the wide sea of potato plants, he was puzzled by their strange appearance.

Instead of a rich, dark green, the leaves were now a sickly whitish color. When he nibbled a leaf it was even more bitter than he had remembered. He tried

18

a juicy center leaf but the strange new bitterness was there too. His twin sister seemed to be having the same trouble, and even Mother Deer did not seem to relish the plants as she had before.

The wise old leader snorted and stamped about in great displeasure. When she noticed that some of the yearlings continued to eat in spite of the bad taste, she ran among them waving her flag as if in sudden alarm. She then dashed back into the woods.

The rest of the herd tagged along out of respect for her position as guardian of the band, but it was evident that some were reluctant to leave their feeding as long as there was no apparent danger in sight.

That night Scrub's stomach chalked up another lesson he would not soon forget. Never again would he take a second bite of a plant that had that strange bitter taste.

Before morning, two of the yearlings that had eaten too hurriedly were so paralyzed they could not even stand. At dawn they were not able to follow the rest of the band to new feeding grounds. The depleted little herd had once again suffered loss at the hand of modern man, and his "inventive genius."

Scrub

Chapter 4: Mother's Choice

After losing the two yearlings to poison potato spray, the deer herd split up even more.

Mother Deer led Scrub and his sister to a field of clover. It was bordered on three sides by woods and brush. On the fourth side, to the north, lay more open fields. Beyond these was a farmhouse - the home of a kindly farmer who enjoyed watching deer browse in his fields.

Somehow the deer seemed to sense the friendliness of the old gentleman. They watched him as he followed his team of horses and rode his tractor over the spreading acres of fields and woods that made up his farm.

For several days Scrub, with his mother and sister, enjoyed the hospitality of the old farm. Early mornings and evening they frequented the clover field. Then during the heat of the long summer days, they enjoyed the cool shade of the woods.

It was quite common for them to meet the kind farmer as he came for his cattle at morning milking time. This was perhaps the most peaceful period of Scrub's early life. For in the life history of wild creatures, danger is the rule rather than the exception.

One mid-summer morning Scrub's pleasant routine was broken by a most dreaded sound - the mixed voices of a pack of neighborhood dogs. What worried Mother Deer most of all was the baying of a hound in the lead. If that dog came across their trail, the little family faced a real danger. When the pack cut across the clover field the doe could wait no longer. The fawns needed a head start, and then some.

Suddenly the lead hound's voice took on a note of real interest. He had hit upon the trail left by the leading deer. They had grazed there in the clover just hours earlier that morning. The farm dogs at his heels smelled nothing. But they well knew that when Old Lop Ears sounded like that, his keen nose had found excitement. Yapping vigorously, they trailed along.

Scrub and his sister bounded along behind their mother, who was well in the lead. They crossed the back pasture in long, easy bounds. At the edge of the woods, Mother Deer seemed to fairly float over the fence. The twins ducked their heads and squeezed between the wires.

Once in the shelter of the brush and trees, the fawns wanted to stop. But the doe urged them on. The voices of the hounds seemed dim and distant to Scrub. How could he know that this dog was very different from other dogs? It would be many hours and many more miles before Old Lop Ears gave up the trail.

Mother Deer slowed her pace in the woods to give the fawns a chance to catch their breath. She also circled and zigzagged to keep the dogs in the woods longer. That would give her a chance to cross more fields without being seen by the dogs as they slowly untangled the trail through the woods.

As the dogs entered the woods on one side, the doe and her twins slipped out the other. They quickly covered another half mile of open fields at full speed.

Low swampy brush land bordered the fields on this side. It was here Mother Deer hoped to throw the dogs off her trail. But even summer with its abundance of food was a disadvantage to the little deer family just now.

There had been no rain for some time, and Mother Deer could not find a large enough expanse of water to cover the trail. The little stream that drained the swamp had dwindled to a series of puddles connected by wet mud. Hopefully at first, then frantically, the doe led her family here and there in search of scent-covering water.

When Mother Deer heard the hound baying across the open fields again, she paused to rest herself and the twins. As the dogs entered the swamp, the doe struck out back across the same fields. Three miles away was a small river that would not be dry. Straight away she led the fawns.

It would take the dogs some time to unravel the twisting trails in the swamp.

Mother Deer's long bounds could devour three miles in short order. Scrub and his sister, however, were tiring of this steady pace. The twins were so blissfully ignorant of their real danger that Mother Deer found it difficult to keep them at top speed.

By the time they reached the river the voice of the hounds could scarcely be heard. Mother Deer waded right in, and the twins were glad to follow. They wanted to just stand and drink while they rested. But the doe headed upstream at a steady walk, sipping a little water as she went.

Scrub and his sister did not want to be left, so they tagged along. But the twins were losing their feeling of urgency. Mother Deer, on the other hand, noticed that the yapping of the hound-led dogs was drawing nearer again. She tried desperately to hurry the fawns. But the twins soon tired of the extra effort necessary to run through the water, and scrambled out on the bank. Mother Deer led them in another twisting, winding trail through brush and cedar thickets, not far from the very place where they had been born.

When the dogs reached the river, they were thrown into momentary confusion. In fact, the farm dogs would have given up the hunt right there. But Old Lop Ears was a born tracker. His baying stopped at the water's edge, where the trail ended.

He crossed the stream and sniffed the far bank, then struck out silently but swiftly up the river's edge.

The old hound soon picked up the trail where the fawns had scrambled out of the water. His deep voice boomed out, calling the scattered dog pack to follow his lead once more.

Mother Deer now faced a desperate peril. Alone, she could have outdistanced the dogs by many miles. But as it was, she must now risk her own life in the uneven race to protect her young.

She tried leading the twins into the brush, then back into the stream. But the exhausted fawns kept climbing out onto the bank before they had gone far enough to throw the old hound off their trail.

Once it appeared the little family had a chance. Old Lop Ears took a wrong turn at the water's edge. When he lost the trail, his voice was always silent. As the silence continued, the doe paused in a secluded thicket to rest herself and her chase-weary fawns.

At the same time, the farm dogs began to lose interest in the seemingly fruitless chase. They began to scatter through the woods in search of some other pursuit. Then one of them ran across the fresh scent of Mother Deer in the thicket. Barking excitedly, he flushed the deer into the open. The chase was now by sight rather than scent. Accordingly, Old Lop Ears found himself trailing far behind rather than leading. A fleeing animal in plain sight was just the kind of sport the farm dogs had been looking for. It couldn't be long now.

Mother Deer and her fawns headed straight away - as fast as their legs would carry them. Scrub and his sister needed no urging from mother now. There was no attempt at strategy at this stage - just speed born of desperation. The race for life led them back toward the farm where the chase had begun some hours earlier, but the first fresh burst of speed was soon over. Even the dogs were beginning to tire a little. Scrub's sister began to lag.

Across the field, the old farmer paused in his garden and leaned on his hoe handle. He didn't like the sounds he had been hearing off and on. Now it was unmistakable. A pack of dogs was running deer across the back of his farm. His experienced ear told him that the dogs were close on their prey. Taking his hoe, the farmer climbed on his tractor and headed for the back pasture.

As he topped the first hill he saw the three deer running - weakly now - like a slow motion picture. Putting the tractor in "road gear", he opened the throttle. The doe seemed to sense that help was coming. She turned quickly to meet the farmer and his tractor.

But two of the dogs closed in on the trailing fawn. With a bleat of pain she stumbled under their weight. Mother Deer wheeled about just as a third dog made a pass at Scrub. She hesitated a split second. How could she defend them both? She struck at Scrub's attacker. He reeled away from her sharp hooves.

Scrub's sister struggled to her feet with her flank torn open and bleeding badly. Mother Deer seemed to concentrate all her efforts now on saving Scrub. She led him straight for the farmer's tractor as the dogs made another rush at the already stricken fawn.

So engrossed were the dogs in their catch that the tractor was right among them before they were aware of it. The farmer soon made his presence known with a steel-bladed hoe. Shouting loudly, he thumped at the surprised dogs until they gladly surrendered their catch - to save their own hides.

The stricken fawn, relieved of her tormentors, submitted trembling but unresisting as the farmer lifted her up to his shoulder. He climbed back onto his tractor and headed back to his barn.

The dogs fled in the opposite direction, leaving Scrub and his mother to themselves. The weary twosome lost no time in seeking shelter and rest from their ordeal. Scrub's sister never did rejoin them.

As dusk drew on that evening Mother Deer led her remaining offspring toward the east. She would quit this land of plenty with its clover fields and ever-present farm dogs.

The twosome traveled slowly, foraging as they went. But steadily and surely they left the farm

27

country behind. At the end of two days, Scrub found himself in a rolling, sandy country.

The land was covered with a scrubby second-growth of poplar, oak and pine. The soil was too poor for profitable farming. There were miles of the rolling hills. Best of all, there were no houses, and no dogs.

Scrub was disappointed in the food supply, however. There was no comparison between his new fare and the farmer's clover fields. But the food was plentiful, such as it was. As autumn drew near, Scrub discovered acorns. They were a new food, but very nourishing.

The remaining few weeks of summer passed in relative peace. Scrub became increasingly independent, and grew into a fine young deer. By autumn he was completely weaned and quite able to take care of himself.

But he still traveled with his mother. Occasionally they encountered other deer. But Mother Deer chose not to join a herd.

There were coyotes in the area, and the deer knew it. But as food was plentiful at this season, the coyotes did not molest the deer. It would be a different story when winter came. The winter - with its cold and hunger.

Chapter 5: Where's Mother?

October with its frosty nights and sunny days was a delight to Scrub. Acorns were plentiful. They put real meat on his bones, giving him strength and stamina. He would be needing all the reserves he could acquire, because winter snows would soon cover most of his food supply.

One chilly morning Scrub awoke to find that Mother Deer had slipped quietly away without waking him. He sniffed the spot where she had slept, and found it nearly cold. Suddenly, Scrub did not feel big or independent anymore. He wanted his mother. Scrub put his nose to the ground and struck out trailing the doe, much as a hound would do. The trail led back in the general direction of the farm country where Scrub had spend the early summer with his little family. As the sun rose, the frost melted away and Scrub lost his mother's trail.

Since he was hungry anyway, Scrub stopped to nibble some "popple" sprouts. Then he wandered around until he found an oak that was shedding a good crop of acorns. Scrub ate his fill, then lay down to rest. Towards evening, he began to feel thirsty. Not knowing the area well, he drifted instinctively down hill.

He had not gone far when he encountered other deer moving steadily in one direction. They seemed

29

to know where they were going, so Scrub followed at a discreet distance. Within a mile he came to a clear stream, fed by several flowing springs.

After drinking, Scrub stayed in the area for some time. He noticed many deer coming and going. But he still felt alone and left out of things.

Scrub moved about, looking and sniffing. But he found no trace of his mother. He bedded down in a dense clump of cedar near the stream and slept. In the morning, Scrub drank from the stream again. Then he struck out resolutely in the direction his mother had taken the day before. He would go back to the farmland.

That night Scrub was back in familiar territory. The next morning found him grazing in an orchard near the farm where his sister had met disaster. Here he made a happy discovery - windfall apples.

All Scrub remembered of this orchard was good grass. Now the ground was covered with juicy, ripe fruit. It tasted so good, the young buck almost forgot he was alone and looking for Mother Deer. Scrub ate until he could hold no more. Then being in an exploratory mood, he squeezed through the fence and stepped out into the road.

There, almost in front of him, was the farmer's daughter. She carried an armful of books, and was on her way to school. Scrub stopped short, ready to flee.

But the girl didn't bark or jump at him. She just kept walking slowly. She spoke to him in a soft, pleasant voice, and Scrub stood his ground. But when the girl reached out her hand as if she wanted to touch him, he wheeled suddenly away and darted back through the fence. The girl went on in happy excitement, to tell her classmates how she had almost "petted a deer".

Scrub sought out a secluded place in the woods, and slept most of the day. That evening he remembered a wonderful tasting white block in the back cow pasture. Later, as he enjoyed the salty treat, Scrub heard a snort behind him.

Whirling, he found himself facing a white tail buck. The buck shook his antlered head, and Scrub backed hastily away. As the buck advanced to take over the salt block, Scrub noticed several does. They were waiting respectfully in the shadows, farther back.

Suddenly he caught a familiar scent. Mother Deer! Scrub circled the buck and bounded to meet his mother. She recognized him, and rubbed his nose. But Scrub was disappointed at the coolness of his reception. As if to add insult to injury, the old buck charged him. One sweep of his antlers knocked Scrub over and sent him rolling. Mother Deer looked on calmly, without even coming to his rescue. After all, sooner or later Scrub must learn the rules of deer etiquette.

For the next few weeks, the young deer was a "hanger-on-about-the-camp". The old buck tolerated him at a distance, realizing that Scrub did not yet pose any real threat to his position.

For Scrub's part, he could not figure out for the life of him why his mother wanted to hang around with that old buck. The buck was not a good leader. He was even careless. In fact, he depended on the does to warn him of approaching danger. Then, too, he was selfish and ill-tempered. He always took first place at the salt block or watering hole. And if one of the does found especially good grazing, he didn't hesitate to crowd her out of it.

Yet, with all his faults, the buck was big and handsome. More important, he could whip any other buck that dared show himself. And the does considered him very acceptable indeed. They cared not at all that each was only one of many wives.

None of this made sense to Scrub yet. How could he know that someday, he too would be a big, handsome, and rather selfish bully?

Chapter 6: Apples and Shotguns

As far as Scrub was concerned, he would gladly have quit this new herd. Except for one thing. He felt more secure with his mother in sight, even if she did pay him little heed. And since Mother Deer seemed bound to tag along with the buck, Scrub followed too - at a safe distance. As he followed, he continued to grow, and learn.

The learning proved to be even more vital than the growing. For he must contend with poacher's high powered rifles, farmer's potato spray, and speeding cars and trucks. There was danger all around, for which size and strength were no defense.

One thing Scrub did have in common with the old buck - an appetite for apples. Nearly every evening the big buck and his harem would spend some time at an old abandoned orchard.

Nearby was an equally old, abandoned house. Along one edge of the orchard, and in front of the house, ran a little-used road. On the other side of this was the woods, and beyond that, the swamp. In fact, it was the very swamp where Scrub and his sister had been born just the spring before.

There were other "fawn followers" of the herd. These youngsters had the same reasons as Scrub - their mothers were part of the old buck's band of does.

Scrub

The fawns had great sport at the orchard. It didn't take many apples to fill their stomachs. Then they would frolic in the old road, like a group of children playing tag. One evening the herd came to the orchard as usual, and ate as usual. Then the fawns began to frolic as usual. The old buck was unusually attentive to the does. None seemed to have a thought for danger. Moonlight flooded the scene and frost sparkled on the grass. It was nearing mid-November. Suddenly the old house belched fire and thunder.

Scrub and his young friends leaped from the road into the brush. The older deer must cross part of the orchard, a fence, and a road before they reached cover. One doe fell at the edge of the apple trees. The buck cleared the fence in a last great leap, then sprawled dead in the middle of the road.

Two "violators" slipped out of the old farm house. They liked to get their venison early - before the big rush of deer season spoiled the easy picking. The doe would make good eating. And the buck, he would bring a good price from a hunter who failed to shoot his own on opening day.

Of course, if a conservation officer happened along, they would be in for trouble. But then, officers couldn't be everywhere at once.

In the darkness and confusion of their flight, the remaining deer scattered through the woods and swamp. When at last Scrub felt safe, he was all alone once more. Finally he bedded down near a clump of "shin-tangle", a low, scrubby juniper that deer consider good eating. Once again, Scrub had been fortunate. He had lived to profit by the misfortune of his companions.

Scrub

Chapter 7: Boys and a Beagle

Next morning, Scrub nibbled at the shin-tangle. Then he wandered off in the general direction of the river. He was not very thirsty, since everything he ate was wet with the morning frost. By mid-morning, the day was getting warm. It was a typical Indian Summer day. Scrub began to move more directly toward the river, with the intention of getting himself a drink. He came to a logging road leading to the river, and trotted down it.

The steady rhythm of a car motor hummed in the distance. Scrub became startled when the sudden grinding of gears interrupted the humming engine. He knew that a car had turned off the road, and that could mean only one thing. It was coming down the trail behind him. Scrub turned and looked back. The car approached steadily but slowly. Nothing to cause alarm, but experience told him to exercise caution. Just a few light bounds, and Scrub was safely hidden behind a branch of brush where he could watch without being seen.

As the car neared the place where Scrub had left the road, it slowed to a halt. A man stepped out, and behind him, a small hound dog. The man pointed. The dog sniffed. Then he sung out in his excited beagle voice.

That song brought back memories to Scrub. He bounded away, intent on putting distance between himself and the hound. He didn't need Mother Deer's urging this time. In just a few minutes, Scrub held a commanding half-mile lead over the beagle. Unfortunately, he couldn't hold that pace for long.

Sensing this, Scrub began to twist and double back as his mother had taught him. However, he was not quite as clever at this as his mother had been. When he heard the hound's voice drawing closer, he panicked and headed straight for the river.

As luck would have it, in so doing he cut across his own trail just ahead of the howling hound. The little beagle was quick to scent the fresher track and swung in close on Scrub's heels. The young buck had lost all the time he spent twisting and doubling. Another burst of speed soon left the eager little hound far behind, but Scrub was filled with new fright at having lost his first gain so quickly.

Once more, he made straight for the river. On reaching it, Scrub splashed in and headed upstream. This might have worked, except for the presence a die-hard trout fisherman. He was having a last "fling" on this Indian Summer day. Scrub rounded a bend in the stream just as the fisherman made a cast. The swinging of the rod and the whine of the reel - not to mention the line lashing towards him, were just too much for Scrub.

The hound was forgotten for the moment. Scrub leaped up the bank and sprinted back towards the place where he had entered the water. The young beagle met him there, sniffing the water's edge and wondering what to do next. He was surprised to see Scrub bearing down on him!

A deer running in full flight was one thing. One charging at the little dog was quite another. He was an inexperienced pup and right now his only thought was to get back to his master. Yelping with fright, the beagle scrambled up the bank. The yelp brought Scrub to a stiff-legged, sliding halt. He was nose-to-nose with the dog as it broke over the river's edge. One great leap carried Scrub across the stream. His white flag rose and fell as he cleared brush, logs, and stumps.

At the sight of the retreating white flag, the beagle's courage rose to new heights. He swam the stream and clambered out on the bank. Once more the chase was on. This was the biggest and fastest "cotton tail" he had ever seen in all his "beagle dreams". And he meant to drive it within range of his master's gun. The master, however, had no intentions of shooting Scrub. He only wanted to train his dog to drive deer for possible use later on.

If only Scrub had known that this young pup couldn't harm him! But past experience had taught the young buck that dogs were to be feared.

By this time he was so frightened and confused that he forsook all attempts at strategy. His only thought was to run. Each time the beagle got close to him, Scrub put on a new burst of speed. And each time, the spurt was shorter than before. The worry and fear were telling on Scrub, even more than the physical strain. The dog was persistent for a pup. After two hours of hopeless twisting and dodging, Scrub still had not shaken him off.

In the meantime, the beagle's owner became uneasy. After all, it was illegal to run deer with dogs. When he heard another car approaching, he decided his hound could find his way home alone. The man got in his car and quit the area.

As he drove out of the woods, the approaching car drove in. It was loaded with boys. On this sunny day, their teacher had brought them out to gather pine stump kindling for their school stove.

The car left the track and wove its way in among a scattering of charred pine stumps. As it stopped, the boys piled out and spread over the area, collecting pine knots and pieces of dry blackened stumps. Suddenly, one of the boys straightened and stared. Excitement and wonder combined on his face. Right among them bolted a young deer. His tongue was out, and he was running with great effort. Even as the boys stared they heard the voice of a young hound not far off. They knew he was coming their way.

Exchanging glances, as if they had rehearsed for it, each boy grabbed a stick or pine knot and crouched behind a stump or bush. When the little beagle came within range, he was met by such a hail of sticks and shouts as to unnerve a much larger beast. His frightened yelps, growing fainter and fainter, told any listener he was now on his way home.

For the second time Scrub had turned in desperation to man for protection. They were queer creatures - these humans. A deer could never be sure if a man would shoot, protect, or just ignore him. But for the present, Scrub did not try to figure that out. He was quite content to slump exhausted into a thicket, where he slept for many hours.

Scrub

Chapter 8:
Hunters, Hunters – Everywhere

For a time, Scrub paid no heed to anything. Then as he began to revive, he became aware of disturbing sounds.

There seemed to be cars in unusual numbers. And they were traveling the logging trails. There were human voices, too, and scents. Of course, Scrub did not know that today was November 14, and that tomorrow would be the opening day of deer season. The next two weeks would be an ordeal by fire for deer in general, and for bucks in particular.

As Scrub rested, thirst came with ever-increasing intensity. By dusk he could wait no longer. Carefully he picked his way toward the river, keeping close to brushy cover.

When he neared a spot commonly used by his kind as a drinking place, he found his way barred by cars, tents, and brightly dressed men. After a lengthy detour, Scrub got his drink. Then he sought another resting place deep in the swamp, not far from his birthplace.

Scrub slept well. Constant danger sharpens the wit of nature's creatures, but their sleep is not troubled by worries of the past or future. Daylight would bring worries aplenty.

Scrub

Scrub had barely stretched himself and begun to nibble a cedar bow next dawn, when he was startled by a rifle shot. He moved deeper into the swamp. Another gunshot echoed from a different quarter. Before he could decide which way to turn, there were even more shots. Hunters were opening up on the deer as they moved along their usual runways.

None of the shots were close enough to panic the young buck, at least not yet. But he moved about uneasily - too nervous to eat. Then he caught the scent of deer and heard the sounds of a rapid approach. There was Mother Deer's scent, and Scrub bounded to meet it. The band was not large. Only two does besides Scrub's mother, with a young spike buck and three fawns about Scrub's size. Mother Deer was clearly the leader. She seemed pleased to see Scrub this time. She led the group to a dense secluded spot and lay down. The others followed her example, except for one of the fawns. He moved about nervously sniffing and listening.

Scrub's mother had been through several hunting seasons. She well knew that the safest course was to stay put. The less they moved about, the less chance there was of being seen and shot at. A lack of antlers was small protection.

During the first few days of the season, the deer moved only to get food and water. They ate from the cedar and red dogwoods among which they hid, and drank from pockets of water they found in the swamp.

By this time, deer who had not been killed were all sticking close to cover and moving only when forced to. Many inexperienced hunters now recruited local boys who knew the woods well. The boys served as "beaters" or "hounds". If boys were not available the hunters themselves would take turns "driving".

The drivers would enter the swamp in a long line from the upwind side. On the down wind side, hunters stationed themselves at likely spots for the deer to emerge. The beaters moved steadily through the swamp whooping it up like a pack of hounds. The scent of humans drifting down wind, combined with the noise, was enough to jump any but the most iron-nerved animal. Then as the fleeing deer left the swamp on the far side, they would have to run a gauntlet of bullets, slugs or buckshot.

It was the morning of the fourth day that Scrub heard the hound-like voices of beaters up wind. He jumped to his feet, ready to flee. But Scrub's mother showed plainly by her actions that she had other ideas. Her experienced ears and nose were not easily fooled. She knew those were human "hounds" approaching. To flee would mean running the gunfire game.

Mother Deer led her charges quickly but quietly. There were no flying leaps, no waving of flags - just

45

a strategic route. Following the doe, the little band threaded its way through windfall so dense it would have been impossible to run. Emerging from this tangle of fallen trees, they leaped over a mud sink-hole. Then they dropped, invisible, into clumps of tangled swamp grass growing on island-like hummocks.

Scrub wondered why his mother did not keep them running, but he had learned above all things to trust her judgment. He felt quite secure, knowing she was lying motionless on the hummock of grass.

As the sounds and scents of the beaters drew closer, Scrub's nose and ears twitched. His feet jerked nervously. But he waited for Mother Deer to make the first move. And she did not stir. When the beaters reached the tangled windfall, they walked around it on either side. The whooping grew louder. The "hounds" would make sure nothing remained hidden in the tangle.

Coming around the end of the windfall, one experienced hunter eyed the grassy bog suspiciously. Taking a pine knob from a rotten log, he hurled it toward the deer's hiding place. It splashed into the sink-hole, and Scrub's heart seemed to stick in his throat.

The spike buck could take it no longer. He burst out of the grass and streaked for cover. But he never made it. A shot blast knocked him down. But it was a rear end shot, and not fatal. Back on his

46

feet, he wobbled forward. The hunters shouted and plunged after him. A few seconds later, his crippled hind legs failed to carry him over a marshy bog. Soon the one spike buck collapsed, in the soft muck. Another shot rang through the swamp, and the young buck's life was over.

By this time Scrub's mother was leading the rest of the band back through the windfall. They traveled only a short distance. Then Mother Deer dropped down again, into the thick cover. The little band of deer lay still until darkness made it safe to move about for food and water.

Scrub

Chapter 9: Mixed Blessings

Scrub was growing rapidly. And it was his good fortune to once again be under the tutelage of a wise mother. He had already learned more self-preservation than many a deer would get in a lifetime. Thanks to Mother Deer's wise leadership, Scrub and his companions rode out the rest of the hunting season, safely hidden in their swamp retreat.

Good fortune, combined with hair-breadth escapes, seemed to stay with Scrub for the first year of his life. The winter that followed was a nearly "open" winter. Cold there was, and plenty of it. But a thick coat of hair, a windbreak of brush and trees, and above all a full stomach are all a deer could ask for in order to be comfortable in the coldest weather.

There were no really heavy snowfalls during Scrub's first winter, so it was not necessary for the deer to yard up in the swamps. As food became scarce in one place, the answer was simple. Move to another. This was lucky for the young deer. If snow gets deep enough to cover the low bushes, the older deer clean all the lower branches of the trees. In a deer yard, that leaves the fawns with nothing but snow - and starvation.

Scrub stayed with the band led by his own mother. Although he was completely weaned, he depended on Mother Deer's wisdom for protection.

Her combination of instinct and experience made her well-qualified as a leader. The doe seemed to know just what moves to make to avoid danger, and Scrub soaked up wisdom that would literally save his hide more than a few times.

Among other things, Mother Deer taught Scrub to make use of man's activities to his own benefit. To offset man's guns and dogs there were corn shocks, haystacks, orchards and salt blocks. Primitive deer never enjoyed such luxuries. Even the guns and dogs could be little worse than the wolf packs and panthers that once roamed the country.

On one frosty morning Scrub woke with a start, just at daybreak. The sound of a jeep engine roared in the distance, growing ever louder. The sturdy little vehicle wound its way among the trees right to the edge of the swamp where the deer had spent the night. Scrub was inclined to be frightened, but his mother led her band only a short distance into the swamp.

The jeep stopped near a poplar stand. Scarcely had its motor been silenced when another engine, noisier still, roared into life. This one seemed to operate by spurts - like an angry beast snarling and growling between breaths. Trees began crashing to the ground at regular intervals. These noises, mingled with men's voices, continued off and on during the day.

The new noises made Scrub nervous, but Mother Deer appeared calm and unafraid. Near dusk, the angry-sounding machine grew quiet. Scrub again heard the steadier sound of the jeep motor, growing fainter in the distance. No sooner had the noises died away than the doe led her band back through the swamp to the place where the deer had grazed just that morning. To Scrub's surprise, the stand of poplar stood no longer. Brushy poplar tops lay scattered about between rows of small log piles. Supper was served in abundance, with plenty more left over for breakfast.

This was Scrub's first encounter with the pulp-wood industry. And it seemed like a good thing. Poplar tops high in the air were usually "for the birds" or slow climbing "porkies". But poplar tops on the ground were just the thing for a hungry deer. The tender twigs and buds rated a close second to cedar tips. Continual winter browsing had made cedar tips hard to find, especially for young deer.

That night Scrub bedded down in the snow. He had not a thought for the cold, for he was blessed with a warm winter coat of long hair, a full stomach and a good constitution. For several days the deer continued to come each evening to feed on the fresh cuttings left by the snarling little engines. The lumber-jacks cut a few cedar fence posts along with their pulp-wood and the deer had a royal feast on the trimmings.

The pulp cutters could not help noticing the abundance of deer tracks as they came to work each morning. With the best of luck and a strong back, a pulp-wood cutter makes only a fair living. And these men were not having the best of luck. Business was slack in general. The cutters had been put on a quota - about 80 % of normal production. And they had other expenses. A saw chain had to be replaced. The jeep must have snow treads and the kids at home needed new boots. All this meant very plain "beans and potatoes" at home on the table, without much variety. A venison apiece would be mighty welcome just before Christmas. It would relieve the pressure on the food bill, and the job could be easily done.

There were a couple of young deer in the bunch that would just fit on the jeep. A piece of canvas and a few armfuls of firewood should serve to hide the evidence. So the next evening, when the jeep pulled away as usual, it held only the driver. The other pulp-cutter crouched low in the brush, near the edge of the swamp.

As the deer began to feed, Mother Deer seemed uneasy. The "man-smell" was stronger than usual. She took a few nervous bites, then moved back into the swamp snorting her displeasure. The other does followed her example at once. As for Scrub, he reached for one more mouthful. He hated to give up such good feeding. The light "crack" of a "22" broke the twilight stillness. One of Scrub's young friends leaped up and fell kicking to the snow. For a moment Scrub seemed rooted to the snow beneath him. Then he leaped. At that same instant, he felt a hot streak across his rump as a second "crack" rang in his ears. The cutter had just been in the process of squeezing the trigger on Scrub, when the deer made his lucky leap. The shot that burned Scrub's hindquarters had actually been aimed just below his ear - the same type of brain shot that had dropped the unfortunate first deer.

The jeep driver had been waiting not far away. Hearing the shots, he returned at once. Both men were disappointed in losing Scrub. But half a small deer apiece would still make quite a Christmas dinner. They quickly cleaned Scrub's unlucky young friend. The remains they buried in the snow, throwing brush over the spot. Then getting out their chain saw, they felled a couple of trees so that the brushy tops fell across the area, wiping out any trace of the incident.

Scrub himself carried evidence he could not so quickly erase. The "burned" streak irritated him for days. But it healed up well. And the impression on his memory lasted for life. Thus far in Scrub's experience "easy picking" had always brought acute danger and frequently disaster to some member of his kind. As long as he lived, Scrub approached feeding areas from the down wind side, and only

53

with great caution. This most recent brush with death taught him the difference between the smell of man's presence and the "has been" odor of one who had been there and gone. And because Scrub learned, he lived to learn more. And he lived when others of his kind died for lack of learning. Of course, there were times when his survival was only a matter of chance. If the pulp-cutter had picked Scrub first, his story would have ended on a Christmas dinner platter.

As for Mother Deer, she had never before encountered fire while following up logging. But she too was a quick learner. The experienced doe next led her little band to a cut-over area where pulpwood had been taken out the year before. There, new poplar shoots were within the reach of both old and young, without the danger of the pulp-cutters.

Chapter 10: Fences

Scrub had enjoyed the plentiful "popple", but that was not his first choice of food. Since he was well-fed and strong, the young buck began to range out a little on his own. While this was more dangerous, it also had its advantages. If Scrub found a choice spot by himself, the older deer could not crowd him out as they did when he kept with the herd. So Scrub left the herd for a few hours or even a few days at a time, but not for good. And his self-confidence grew, right along with his body.

The young deer found small patches of swamp where one animal alone could pick up a good meal - with variety. Cedar, shin-tangle, red dogwood - even a few frozen wild apples now and then proved to be tempting fare for Scrub's growing appetite. During winters of heavy snow, this scattered feeding was not available to yard-bound deer in the larger swamps.

After two or three weeks of uneventful foraging, Scrub grew even bolder. He ventured closer and closer to human dwellings. Scrub had learned that he was not likely to be bothered near the home of the old gentleman who had rescued him as a fawn on his tractor. The old farmer had a cattle dog that would bark and run at Scrub. But the dog did not try to follow him into the woods. And at the nearest house cross the road, there was no dog at all.

Between the two dwellings was the orchard where Scrub had stepped out and encountered the farmer's daughter with her armload of books. Just behind the little orchard stretched a mile or more of woods broken by patches of brush, small clearings, a trout stream and two or three not-so-large swampy spots. It was ideal deer range, except it was in the same general area where Scrub and his mother had met near disaster several times.

After each near brush with death, Scrub and Mother Deer had moved to wilder country. But somehow they always came back to the abundant food supply near the farms. Scrub seemed to sense a protective force and kept close to the old farmer's place for several days.

One daybreak found Scrub pawing snow in the little orchard. He was rewarded with a few apples, well-preserved beneath the blanket of white. As daylight increased, Scrub moved into the woods and down to the creek bank where patches of shin-tangle grew. For some unknown reason these bitter little junipers rank as top fare to white tails, right next to real delicacies such as apples. Scrub nibbled here and there. Being well-fed he was quite choosy. He worked his way up to the creek bank, well pleased with the world in general, and looking for a safe, comfortable place to sleep away the day. At the edge of the woods Scrub slipped between the barbed wires of a fence. The barbs plucked out a tuft of hair, but Scrub's thick coat protected him from scratches.

Between this woods and the next, a stream worked its way through a swampy little valley. Beside the stream were a few scrubby cedars, red dogwood brush, a birch or two, and a field of coarse, shoulder-high grass. Snow lay deep in the grass, but it was light and fluffy. Scrub's slender legs moved easily through it. Underneath, the ground was springy and wet. A dog would be literally "snowed under" if he tried to trail a deer through such cover. A man would soon be wet to the waist. Many times in Scrub's life, Mother Deer had led him to such places to bed down for a day or night of undisturbed rest. Now he nibbled his way from bush to cedar, and back to bush again. Finally, the young deer curled up close under the low hanging branches of a small cedar.

Scrub was just comfortably settled when he heard a door slam shut just out of sight, over the nearest rise. Most likely, that would be the nearest neighbor of his farmer friend. Scrub relaxed for more napping. But once again he pricked up his ears - this time at the unmistakable sound of fence wire creaking. Scrub sniffed the air and spread his ears to catch the slightest hint of danger. He detected no scent in the air, and no sound met his ears.

Scrub

Reassured by the tall dead grass about him, Scrub tucked his nose back under his warm flank and slept - relaxed and contented.

While Scrub slept, the farmer's neighbor tramped the woods in a pair of home-made snowshoes. The man carried no gun, but enjoyed "reading" stories left in the snow by his woodland friends.

On this particular morning, the man had crawled through the fence into the woods behind his house. He soon picked up Scrub's trail leading from the orchard toward the creek below the hill. This could be interesting. The track was freshly made and showed the deer to be taking his time. He might be bedded down or browsing just about any place in the brush near the creek. The amateur naturalist followed as quietly as he could, while scanning the woods ahead of him.

Suddenly, Scrub snapped out of his slumber. Wasn't that a squeaking fence wire again? This time it came from the same spot where he had squeezed through barely an hour before. Faintly now, Scrub heard the swishing of snow and brush. The sound came slowly but steadily nearer. No barking, not enough air stirring to carry a scent - it must be a man!

Remembering the past, Scrub decided to play the still act. This being his first winter, Scrub did not realize that with snow on the ground a man's eyes are as good as a hound's nose. During the recent hunting season Scrub and his mother had lain still while hunters passed on either side. He would try it again. Scrub made himself as small as possible and waited. As the swishing footsteps drew close the young deer's feet twitched and his tail began to jerk. Then he could hold his head down no longer. Scrub peeked through the branches and grass, catching a glimpse of the man's head bobbing up and down. He was turning here, pausing there, just as Scrub had done. The man stopped where Scrub stopped to note just what the deer liked best to eat.

As his follower moved to circle Scrub's cedar the young deer burst out of his cover like a frightened partridge. He bounded away with low, ghost-like strides - taking advantage of the tall grass for cover. A few leaps, and Scrub reached the wire fence again. Not wanting to expose himself by a high leap, Scrub ducked his head to scoot under the grass- level barbed wire. But his dive under the wire ended abruptly in a jarring, neck-twisting jerk.

Rusting away in the tall grass lay a broken down, woven wire fence. It snagged Scrub much the same as a gill net might to catch a fish. The momentum of the young deer's leap drove his head and neck tightly into the fence, while his body flipped over on top of his own head. And the weight of his body pushed Scrub's nose down even farther into the water and mud of the swamp.

Scrub

The man watched, surprised and excited, wondering if he should try to help free the struggling young deer. But Scrub soon solved the problem himself. After a few aimless flounders he regained his footing, jerking his head loose. Scrub took a quick jump backwards, then with a mighty leap soared over the low-lying fence that had trapped him. Several fences formed a corner near the spot where Scrub had tangled. He had no more than cleared the first fence, when he was faced with another. Again the young buck leaped - as if he were reaching for the sky. If the fence had been twice as high, Scrub would have cleared it with room to spare.

Many a deer before Scrub had been entangled in that and other fences. If Scrub had died in the fence, he would not have been the first deer to reach the end of the road in that way. Once again, Scrub was impressed with the fact that man's abundance always seemed to be coupled with mankind's hazards.

In spite of the dangers of fences, at least they could be counted on not to chase him. They could be counted on to stay in the same place. He simply had to make allowances for them in his travels. From that day on, Scrub cleared all fences with room to spare when running. When walking at his leisure, he might still step or crawl between the strands of a barbed wire fence. But there would be no more running through or diving under.

Chapter 11: Back to Mother

After his encounter with the fence, Scrub took the shortest route back to the big swamp where he had last seen Mother Deer. For the rest of the winter, he stayed close to the little band of deer she led.

The coming of Spring found Scrub a husky yearling. True, he had been born ahead of season. The odds had been great against him. But Mother Deer's wisdom, combined with good fortune, had tipped the balance in Scrub's favor. From now on his chances of survival were as good as for any of his kind - and better than most. For he had experienced the best of training. On top of that, he had lived to profit by the experience of some of his less fortunate companions, who had perished by the way.

As the snow melted, Mother Deer led her band to upland woods bordering the potato farmer's rye fields. Early morning and late evening found the deer enjoying this welcome change of diet, after a winter of brushy eating.

Then one day Scrub wandered from the herd again. When he returned at evening feeding time, Mother Deer had disappeared. Scrub joined the others in the rye field. By the next morning, only Scrub and two other yearlings remained in the little band. The does had slipped away quietly, one by one, to find secluded spots to drop their fawns.

The three yearlings stuck together. It gave them a sense of security, if nothing else. They had learned by this time that three sets of eyes, ears, and nostrils were better than one for detecting the approach of danger. Scrub soon assumed leadership of the other two yearlings.

One early June morning the three youngsters visited the salt block in the friendly farmer's pasture. Here Scrub detected a familiar scent. Just a short distance away stood Mother Deer. The reunion resembled a similar meeting just one year earlier. Only this time, Scrub was the yearling. A spotted fawn trotted close to Mother Deer's heels. While Mother Deer seemed pleased to see Scrub, it was plain that the fawn now claimed first place in her affections. As Scrub sniffed inquiringly at the little fellow, Mother Deer stamped her feet. Sensing her warning, Scrub backed quietly away.

Within a few days the other yearlings had found their mothers again. The band of deer had at one time numbered six, then three. Now there were ten - thanks to two single fawns and one pair of twins. Scrub began to share the position of leader with Mother Deer, although her decisions were still final. Scrub became a self-appointed sentinel. His senses developed to the point where Mother Deer depended on him to give warning of any unusual scent or sound. Then she would indicate how to react.

Hasty flight was a last resort. Mother Deer's reaction to a hint of danger was always to freeze. Movement attracts attention, and the less attention the better. This was especially true with fawns in the band. Once the source of danger was located, Mother Deer acted quickly to avoid it.

Often she led her charges quietly to the nearest brushy cover, where they all dropped out of sight. In most cases the deer remained hidden, and unnoticed. A farmer or woodsman might pass within a few yards of their hiding spot, and never guess their presence.

The summer progressed, with its usual fare of adventure. Twice the band had serious brushes with a pack of dogs. When Scrub and Mother Deer learned that dogs were on their track, they made no attempt to hide. Speed, cunning, and endurance were the essential elements here.

A half dozen dogs were chasing rabbits through the swamp one evening. By chance, the rabbit's twisting trail crossed that of the little deer herd. Scrub and his companions had just crossed the swamp after getting their evening's drink at the trout stream. The scent of a whole band of deer promised more excitement than a single cottontail, and the pack of dogs quickly took up the chase.

The deer were just moving out of the area, when their sharp ears caught the sound of dogs chasing a rabbit. A sudden chorus of yappings and howls told Scrub and the band that the dogs had picked up their trail. Now Mother Deer sprang into a straight-away lead. Her fawn could match her speed for a short time, and she meant to make the most of it. As soon as the fawn began to lag, Mother Deer made a sharp turn. Scrub followed close. Some of the band made the turn, but some kept on. Soon Mother Deer twisted again. After a few more such turns, the band of deer was scattered - each moving in different directions.

The scattering was deliberate on the part of the doe. If the dogs scattered, it would give the does a better chance to defend their fawns against a diminished group of dogs. If the dogs stuck to one track, at least part of the herd would escape.

This time the dogs scattered, one here, another there. Once separated, they began to give up the chase, one at a time. However, they had gotten the excitement of the chase in their blood. Scrub knew they would be watching for another chance.

In the early dawn the deer left the salt lick, and went to graze with some cattle in a clover field. That turned out to be the morning the friendly farmer had planned a big day's work. He sent his two cattle dogs out early, to bring in the cows for milking. As the dogs neared the herd of cattle, they barked to start them on their way to the barn. White flags waving, the deer bounded over the nearest fence and into the woods. The dogs forgot their immediate duty, and gave chase. But they were not particularly dangerous, and soon returned to their neglected cows.

Unfortunately for the herd of deer, the excited barking of the cattle dogs had attracted some unwanted attention. A pack of hunting dogs, this time including Old Lop Ears himself, came to investigate. Soon a grim chase was on.

It was in the same general area where Scrub's twin sister had met disaster the summer before. This time the band, led by Scrub and Mother Deer, found water in the nearest swamp. It threw the dogs into temporary confusion and gave the deer a good lead. After leaving the wet swamp, Scrub's mother used the scattering tactic again. It proved successful, at least as far as her own family was concerned.

Old Lop Ears patiently skirted the swamp until he heard where the deer had come out. Then he picked up the trail again. His deep, howling voice kept the pack of dogs united. As the deer scattered, the hound with his pack followed the straightest lead. They finally wore down one young doe and her fawn. The doe put up a mother's fight, and was badly bitten. But the odds were too great. While part of the pack held the doe at bay, the others made short work of her fawn. When she knew the fawn was dead, the doe fled for her own life.

This was the second time in a week that dogs had scattered the band of deer. Now that the hound had joined the pack, Scrub's mother made no attempt to bring the deer together again. Neither did she join another band. She would take her fawn to wilder country as she had done with Scrub the year before. Scrub elected to follow.

Mother Deer made no attempt to keep Scrub with her. He was welcome - as long as he kept his distance from her fawn. For two days the threesome traveled away from the fertile farm country. Then they came to an abandoned farm homestead. It boasted a few broken down old apple trees, some brushy fence rows, and a field or two of quack grass. The rolling hills surrounding the clearing were covered with scrubby oak, jack pine and poplar.

At the back end of the place a small swamp with an even smaller spring provided water enough for the deer. It seemed an ideal location. Occasionally a logging truck or a car stirred up a cloud of dust on the little-used dirt road that skirted the edge of the old farm. The nearest human habitation was far away. Not the faintest sound of barking dogs reached the keen ears of Scrub, or his mother.

Chapter 12: Poachers!

Scrub soon made new acquaintances. The few deer in the area frequented the watering hole at the back of the old homestead. In the late evening, deer from the oak woods came to graze or romp in the open fields of quack grass.

One moonlit night Scrub romped with another yearling while Mother Deer, shadowed by her fawn, grazed near the road. The purr of a car motor and the approach of lights caused the deer to freeze - heads up - eyes toward the road. The car was moving slowly.

Suddenly a bright beam of light swept across the field. Pin points of amber glowed as the deer's eyes reflected the glare of the spotlight. As the sweeping light fell on Scrub's mother, the car braked to a stop. The light seemed to hold Mother Deer spellbound. But the squeak of a car door released her. Almost at the same instant she leaped, the blast of a shotgun rent the night air.

The charge of the buckshot aimed between her glowing eyes shattered a front leg instead of Mother Deer's skull. The leap had saved her life, but her leg was worse than useless.

White flags bobbed as the herd made for the oak woods. Scrub's mother ran awkwardly. Her hind legs still sent her sailing in long leaps, but her right front leg flopped about in any direction. Each time the doe struck the ground, she stumbled. At the edge of the field, the dangling leg caught in the fence-row brush. Mother Deer somersaulted, then landed dazed and sprawling in the edge of the woods. The weight of her body snapped the fragments of skin that had held the shattered bone. Mother Deer's leg was gone just above the knee.

Since the deer's lower leg is not fleshy, there was not a great loss of blood. Mother Deer's fawn soon found her lying there, and snuggled down beside her. The doe still had something to live for. The weather was mild and food plentiful.

Next morning Scrub returned to the spring to drink. Before he had finished, his mother hobbled painfully to the edge of the swampy spot. She drank from the nearest puddle she could reach. Then she grazed briefly, and lay down in a brushy spot. The injured doe had little milk for her fawn.

The fawn seemed to realize that something was wrong. As Scrub moved about, feeding at the edge of the woods, the fawn followed him. It was big enough to eat grass and leaves, so it would not starve.

Scrub himself would always connect engine noise with danger. He avoided roadsides and fled at the approach of any motor sound.

Mother Deer kept close to the watering spot for many days. She moved about only enough to drink and feed. She allowed the fawn to nurse a little each day. But much of the time the youngster spent with Scrub. The yearling grew quite fond of his little brother, and took care to keep him out of danger and trouble.

After two weeks Mother Deer began to move about a little more. She avoided open spaces or any other possible danger spots. Never again did she attempt to join a band of deer or to assume leadership. Her one purpose seemed to be to find security for her fawn and herself. While Scrub did not stay by his mother constantly, he did keep track of her. By now, the young buck was as large as Mother Deer. He even sprouted antlers - after a sort.

Scrub

Chapter 13: Courtship

Dawn streaked the October sky. Scrub rose, stretched, and shook the frost from his coat. It was good to be alive. Mother Deer and her fawn were sleeping not far away. Feeling the urge to wander, Scrub struck out in a mood for adventure. A pair of well-curved, two-pronged antlers now graced his head. It had been slightly over a year and a half since his birth in the snow-bound cedar swamp.

This early autumn morning Scrub headed for a distant watering place he had visited the fall before. Then he had been a lonely, six-months fawn looking for his mother. Now he knew not what he was looking for - only that he was looking. It was full daylight as Scrub drew near the bubbling springs. They were located at the end of a deep ravine, and formed the headwaters of a good-sized trout stream.

At the edge of the ravine Scrub paused. Below him a group of deer about his own age had finished drinking. They seemed playful. Scrub snorted lightly and bounded down the bank. The group scattered, then turned to eye the newcomer. Scrub drank before he attempted to join them. His thirst quenched, Scrub advanced to try his fortune among the group. One young buck about his own size made a threatening move, but when Scrub held his ground, the other buck backed off. Then Scrub was accepted by the whole group, although just like in a group of teenagers, he could be neither sissy nor bully.

Scrub had not been with his new friends more than a few minutes when he noticed a doe who was plainly trying to attract attention. His ears perked in interest. Slowly he advanced to within nose-rubbing range. The young twosome's noses touched just once. Then the fickle doe whirled and bounded lightly up a slope. But she didn't go far. Scrub followed, and so did his rival. As a newcomer, Scrub would either have to fight, or forget his new interest.

The two young bucks squared away. Antlers whacked and hooves thumped. Physically the match was even, but Scrub was more determined. The other buck soon decided this romance wasn't worth the effort - not at the present, anyway.

Scrub snorted defiantly and turned to take possession. The teasing young thing had moved further up the slope. Scrub overtook her just as she reached the top of the ravine. Just at that moment, a full-fledged, antlered buck burst out of the scrub-oak. He had been attracted by the rattle of antlers. To this experienced monarch the sound of combat spelled "doe" for the victor. And he was in the habit of being the victor.

Having tasted victory himself, Scrub was not inclined to flee. But he might as well have been.

One swoop of the big buck's antlers sent Scrub sailing down the bank he had just ascended. The big fellow made no attempt to press the quarrel, and Scrub knew when he was licked. The doe shed no tears for Scrub. She trotted off with the old buck at her heels, as if she had been expecting him all along.

Scrub's first attempt at courtship had brought a short but varied experience. First there was the awakening of new interests. Then the contest, triumph, and short-lived possession of the treasure. Now he stood at the bottom of the ravine, beaten and disillusioned. Romance was for the birds, and big bullies. He was all through. And then again, maybe not. Another young doe was approaching the watering hole.

Scrub

Chapter 14:
Hunter With a Soft Spot

Scrub began to feel he had "arrived" in the deer world. He had antlers of a sort, and scars of various descriptions. He had fought, and, win or lose, he was still game. He had even mated - between maulings from the big bucks. And now it was mid-November - the 15th to be exact. It was opening day again. And a veritable army of hunters opened fire on the deer herd that blustery winter day.

It was to be an "any deer" season. Bucks, does, fawns - all were legal game. Hunting restrictions combined with last season's mild, open winter had increased the deer population to the saturation point. According to the game experts, if all the does and fawns were left in the woods, their winter food supply would be gone by January. After that two months of starvation would follow. If the winter happened to be open again, the deer might pull through. But the problem would only be more serious the next year.

An "any deer" season, they claimed, would reduce the herd to a smaller number. This in turn would leave the remaining deer more food per deer during the critical winter "yard up".

75

Scrub

Of course, Scrub and his fellows understood nothing of this argument. But Scrub did know that he was one frightened deer during that opening day. He suddenly wanted his mother again and promptly set out to find her. It was not difficult. She and her fawn kept close to the small water hole where they had spent the early part of the summer. Since losing her leg, Scrub's mother had avoided travel. She was not in good condition and this fall she had shown no interest in a buck.

Now she seemed glad to see Scrub again. They had come to depend on each other in times of danger. Mother Deer had trained Scrub well, and now he could be of help to her in detecting scents and sounds of danger.

A group of hunters had made camp not far from the old deserted homestead. They had noticed the orchard gone wild. It had a fair crop of wormy apples. Knowing the deer's liking for apples, the hunters camped just far enough away to avoid scaring the deer away before the first shots could be fired.

On opening morning, the men had laid in the grass on the downwind side of the apple trees. The result was quite a success from the standpoint of meat taken. A couple of fawns would be eaten in camp. It would be too humiliating to take the little carcasses home on a fender. No antlers had been taken in the kill, at least not so far.

Surviving deer fled to the woods and swamps. Mother Deer and her fawn had not been among the group under the apple trees, but she had been close enough to be badly frightened by the gunfire. She did not flee, but dropped with her fawn into the nearest thicket and stayed put. That night she met Scrub at the water hole.

Everything seemed peaceful enough by night. Scrub followed his mother and her half-grown fawn into the oak woods. Acorns were plentiful enough, so they need not expose themselves in an open field to get good food.

The hunters knew it would be useless to try another ambush at the orchard. Two more deer would fill all their licenses. They hoped to get at least one good buck with a rack. So they decided on a "drive".

The oldest member of the party was a crack shot, but not equal to the rigors of driving. He was chosen to sit at the end of the "gauntlet". The hunters hoped to drive any deer in the area out through a ravine with a ridge on each side.

"Hounds" in the form of limber-legged boys whooped it up through a whole section of land. The hunters stationed themselves in a spreading "v" along the two ridges with the old veteran at the point. It was hoped that the deer could be funneled out past him.

Scrub

At dawn of the second day Scrub heard the distant chorus of voices. Mother Deer too heard, and knew what was coming. She moved quietly, without haste. The beaters were far off. The deer would have time for a cautious retreat. No bounding leaps or waving flags were to attract attention. The three deer picked their way carefully, keeping close to brushy cover. They moved toward the ravine as that was the only way to avoid crossing open fields. The bottom of the ravine itself was open, but the deer clung to the brushy cover along the edge. Eventually, the ravine led to a swamp that would discourage most hunters.

The trio slipped quietly along downwind. A sudden shift of air currents brought the scent of man, strong and close. They had almost bumped into the old sportsman sitting motionless with his back against a scrubby jack pine.

The hunter spotted Mother Deer's ears at about the same instant she scented him. Then Scrub's antlers appeared above a clump of sumac just beyond the doe.

There was no time for strategy on either side. The hunter leaped to his feet to see over the brush, and the deer bounded full speed ahead. The old man was not interested in the fawn. He wanted the young buck, but the doe blocked that shot. He must drop her first to get a clear shot at Scrub.

With a steady hand, the veteran hunter leveled on a small clearing the deer must cross. As the three of them burst out of the brush, he wondered at the queer gait of the doe. His sights lined on her right shoulder, then he noticed the healed stump of her leg.

His sporting instinct admired courage. That doe had just about had her share of troubles. The fawn needed her and she needed the fawn. The hunter purposely raised the gun barrel as he squeezed the trigger. The wild shot lent wings to Scrub's legs. The hunter leaned against a tree, and sighed.

The young buck didn't have much of a rack anyway. He could tell the fellows the bullet was deflected by brush.

It was no matter of instinct or wisdom that spared Scrub and his mother this time. Pure luck dictated that the deer family meet a sportsman with a heart - a heart that had a soft spot for a handicapped old doe that was still game. Had he dropped the whole family, though, they would have gone out the "easy way". For nature herself would show neither sporting instinct nor mercy in the cold, hungry months to come.

Scrub

Chapter 15:
Deep, White - and Everywhere

The end of the "any deer" season found Scrub, with his mother and the now half-grown fawn, still among the living. But unlike a deer's life the previous winter, it was no easy living.

The numbers of deer had been reduced sharply by the recent hunting season. However, the winter food supply had been over browsed the year before. This winter the snow came early - and stayed. By the end of December the depth of snow had eliminated all grass or acorns from the fare. The deer in the oak woods had to move into the evergreen swamps or travel to poplar and hardwood country. Tops from logging and pulpwood operations helped provide food through the next month.

Then one morning, Scrub awoke to find himself quite warm and comfortable under a 16-inch blanket of fresh snow. He rose and shook himself. The temperature was not severe, and the snow was light and fluffy. It was not too difficult for the young buck to move about - slowly. Before this latest snowfall, there had already been plenty of snow. Now Scrub's belly barely cleared the top of it. Mother Deer had a little trouble because of her missing leg. The fawn pushed snow with its chest as it moved forward.

Due to the inclement weather, the pulp-cutters and loggers gave up. The snow was just too deep to keep wallowing from tree to tree. Equipment either bogged down or broke down. It would be cheaper for them to sit until spring.

Any deer who were not in the evergreen swamps made a quick beeline in that direction. Under the evergreens, the snow was not quite so deep. Soon there were beaten paths interlaced all through the swamp where Scrub had "yarded up" with his mother and the fawn.

Scrub fared not too badly. Even the doe and her fawn made out for the first two weeks. There were probably fifteen or twenty deer in the same swamp. Each day the deer browsed on the cedar boughs that were easiest to reach. Soon the fawns of the previous spring were stretching to their limit, trying to get a bite here and there.

Then the real cold set in. Below-zero temperatures followed night after night. With plenty of food the cold was easy to take, but on empty or half-filled stomachs the youngsters fat reserves soon disappeared. Even the older deer found it necessary to rear on their hind feet to reach the dwindling food supply. Mother Deer had entered the yard with little reserves to draw on. She became too weak and shaky to browse while standing on her hind legs.

Her fawn followed her about, being equally weak and wobbly.

Here and there along the edge of the swamp stood a few bushy cedars apart from the others. They offered tempting fare, if only they could be reached. The stronger deer began to push out to reach these few trees. Scrub was able to lunge and rabbit-hop his way out to one of them. The sight of him feasting on the green boughs spurred the doe to follow. Keeping in Scrub's tracks, she made it. The fawn tried next, but could not make the long hops.

Scrub and Mother Deer stripped the young cedar of all edible browse. Then, refreshed and strengthened, they wallowed and hopped back to the yard. As the doe came up to her puffy-cheeked fawn she nudged him momentarily. He made a weak effort to move, then huddled deeper in the snow. The doe pushed on. Personal survival was the only instinct she had left. The fawn was nearly a goner. He would make a bony meal for a scavenging fox or coyote.

Mother Deer herself had eaten her last good meal. Two days later Scrub pushed out towards another solitary cedar. It was much farther. The doe could not make it all the way without resting. A less handicapped deer pushed his way by. By the time Mother Deer arrived, the scrubby tree had been stripped. She chewed at the tough remains, but did not find the strength to take her back to the yard.

Halfway there, she sank into the snow to rest. She slept, and shivered, and slept, and froze.

Scrub and a handful of the original band of deer scoured the "yard", chewing on tough branches that had previously been rejected. They pawed in the air, in an effort to bring down branches that were just out of reach. Things began to look bad, even for the strongest. Then the first signs of spring appeared. The sun shone - the south wind blew, and snow began to melt. But unfortunately, food was still out of reach.

A heavy, wet spring snow came to save the starving herd. It began on a thawing March evening. The sticky stuff clung everywhere. Cedar boughs above the deer's heads began to bend under the weight of the water-logged snow.

It was snow - deep, white, and everywhere, that had bound the deer to the yard with its limited food supply. Now, more snow, wet, clinging, heavy stuff, brought food down in abundance. Lower branches bent to the ground. Tops bent lower and lower - finally snapping and falling to provide ample food to pull the starving deer through the last two or three weeks of the spring break-up. In some cases, whole trees snapped off and lay across the runways of the deer yard. Scrub's bony frame took on new shape and new strength.

Nature had proved most cruel - and then kind. The weak, the old, the handicapped, all had to go.

There was no place for sentiment in her make-up. Next year there would be fewer deer, but more food for the ones that were left.

The following November hunters would claim that the "any deer" season had wiped out the deer. Those who walked through the deer yards after the snow had gone could give a different answer. In many yards, half the deer had been left behind as piles of bones and hair.

Scrub

Chapter 16: The Big Buck

Scrub left the yard alone that spring. He did not join any band of deer, but kept to himself. From now on he avoided company except during mating season.

This summer, Scrub reached his prime in size and maturity. He developed wind and staying power so that he no longer feared the bark of a dog or the howl of the coyote. Except under certain snow conditions, he could outdistance or outfight them. Both instinct and experience taught him to fear man. But that creature's noisy habits and peculiar odor made him easy to avoid.

Scrub made one exception to his "avoiding man" rule. He had no fear of the old farmer who had once saved his life from the pack of dogs. His friend's land was posted against hunting and the buck made it the center of his range. There was rye to be had in late autumn and spring. Clover and corn came in their season - and then there were apples. Of course, there was also the convenient salt block in the back pasture just at the edge of the woods.

Scrub's old enemies, the dogs, soon learned that he was no longer the fearful, insecure, fawn or yearling. He could quickly lose the farm dogs by wading in a swamp or stream, or even by pure speed.

Scrub

Once in late summer Old Lop Ears and his pack pressed Scrub to the limit. He was tired of running in the summer heat. He slackened his pace. An eager young collie dashed ahead of the hound and made a lunge at Scrub's heels as we would at a cow or calf. Scrub whirled, caught the foolish dog on his antlers, and tossed him against a tree. The dog limped for home howling a different tune. Old Lop Ears slid to a halt. Scrub faced him, head lowered. The wise old hound took a good look at the eight velvet-covered points on Scrub's rack. He would go rabbit hunting - right away! The other dogs quickly followed Old Lop Ears example.

Scrub shook himself, snorted, and stamped his feet. A feeling of self-confidence welled up inside him. He had faced his old enemy, the hound, and the enemy had fled. His only real fear now was man, or his devices. Thanks to his mother and good fortune, he was well-equipped to face even that threat to his survival.

Scrub lived and prospered for the next three years. As whitetails go he became an old veteran. Like Job of old, he saw his sons and his sons' sons, even four generations.

A deer in captivity might live to the ripe old age of 20 years, but in the wild a five or six-year-old buck is considered a patriarch.

Scrub was no longer a "scrub" by any means. He became known in his area simply as "The Big

Buck". He traveled little by day and was seldom seen by men. The rare occasions when he was seen were enough to spread his fame afar.

Hunters spent may bone-chilling hours sitting in November's raw cold, hoping for one shot at the big fellow. Scrub's skill at avoiding them seemed almost uncanny.

In mating season Scrub made life miserable for other bucks. He ranged far and wide, smelling out the trails of does who might be looking for a mate. Scrub attacked on sight any buck large enough to be interested in a doe.

By one frosty October morning, Scrub had grown to a five-year old monarch with a ten-point rack. He ran with his nose to the ground, trailing a prospective doe through a cedar swamp. So intent was he on the business at hand, that a nearby partridge hunter went unnoticed.

The man had heard Scrub approaching and stood motionless as the big buck passed within a few feet. The hunter's eyes widened with interest. Then and there he began making plans for a drive that would take the big buck. He was a weekend hunter from the city, but he immediately started to recruit help from among the local farmer sportsmen he knew. A dozen men came to be included in the all-out effort to take "The Big Buck". They would all keep a sharp eye out for the big fellow, as well as a sharp ear tuned to rumors of his whereabouts.

A month later the platoon of hunters met in one cabin to plan the next day's hunt. A school boy, son of one of the men, reported seeing "the biggest deer track you ever saw" crossing the road at the edge of Uncle Walt's swamp pasture. That had been only this morning, as he walked to school.

Uncle Walt was Scrub's farmer friend whose land was posted against hunting. One of the hunters owned an "80" bordering the posted farm. The hunters decided to send unarmed men and boys in a long curving line across the old farmer's place just at daylight. A few of the group would take all the guns and station themselves on the unposted "80". "The Big Buck" would catch it when he crossed the fence.

Chapter 17: The Big Drive

Dawn found the plan progressing on schedule. The hunters had a special advantage that pleased them greatly. A light snowfall had come during the night. Tracing would be excellent. The beaters made a lot of small noises, but omitted the usual hound-like shouts. They did not want to stir up Uncle Walt.

Scrub heard their small noises all right - and he did not like it. He seemed to sense that a trap had been set for him. Instead of sticking to the woods, Scrub leaped into the open and raced for the old farmer's house. Right through the backyard and out the front driveway he bounded. No hunters were waiting there. The Big Buck crossed the road into the small orchard he had frequented so many times. He paused to munch a half frozen apple, then moved on into the woods beyond.

The surprised hunters had no trouble seeing where Scrub went, but they did not dare follow through the farmyard. They did hurry across the back of the farm to tell the waiting gunners what had happened.

Scrub was now in a "section" of square mile with a road on each of the four sides. The hunters quickly climbed into cars. As they drove around the square section they stopped at likely spots to let out the gunners one at a time. Soon Scrub's square of land was completely surrounded. No deer could leave that square mile without being seen or fired upon.

The boys took up the trail where Scrub had entered the orchard. It should be simple to follow the trail in the fresh snow. But they soon found that it did not stay simple.

Scrub was not long in discovering that someone was on his trail. He struck out through a thickly tangled swamp. In some places there was enough water to melt the light snow. The buck circled back on his own trail. Scrub watched from a thicket as the two boys stumbled and plowed through brush that had barely slowed his speed.

Human scent was strong, but there was no scent of gunpowder that usually went with armed hunters. Scrub sensed that these boys were not dangerous in themselves, but he was sure danger waited someplace not far away. He would stick close to the swamp and take a chance on the boys.

The wise old buck began following the boys - at a safe distance. As long as he knew where they were he would be safe from them, at least. The sun rose to sparkle on the newly fallen snow - and to melt large patches of it.

By noon the exhausted boys had made three large circles through the tangled swamp. The snow had melted until they were not sure if they were on

Scrub's track or not. In fact, they were not even sure just where they were. There was nothing to be frightened about, however. It was less than a mile to the road in any direction. The boys sat down to rest and take stock on their situation.

Scrub himself was tired of this game. Since nothing alarming had happened, he wandered deeper into the swamp and lay down behind a huge rotting log.

At about the same time the boys were wondering what to do next, the hunters had gathered on the north side of the square mile. Each expected the other to have some report of The Big Buck, or the boys who were tracking him. When it was learned that neither buck nor boys had been seen, the hunters decided to investigate.

First they honked their car horns and shouted to let the boys know where they were. The boys heard and answered, but because of the wind direction their shouts sounded faint to the hunters. The whole group of men started into the woods to see if the boys needed help. The boys jumped up and started toward the road where they had heard the car horns. Somewhere in between, Scrub lay behind his log. It was an uncomfortable position.

Experience had taught him that if he ran he would probably be shot at. If he stayed put, the hunters would most likely pass right by him without knowing he was there. The plan might fray his nerves, but it had served him well in the past.

93

Closer and closer came the two groups. Each was guided by the shouts of the other. Soon only the swampy thicket that was Scrub's hiding place separated the hunters from the two boys. To avoid the water and mud, the men stopped. They hesitated, then one, impatient of delay, plunged into the brush while the others went around. The brush snapped on the backside of Scrub's leg. Then came a thump on top of it. Scrub could lay still no longer. Scrub saw a boy, arms waving, poised on his log to leap. But Scrub leaped first. The startled boy fell off the log.

Scrub was too unnerved to think of strategy, but he made up for that in desperate speed. A mighty leap carried him out of the brush directly into the group of waiting hunters. The men had been expecting the boys. In the confusion the excited men shot almost at random. Bullets and buckshot clipped brush and trees around, above, and under the fleeing Scrub.

There were some "clippings" pretty close to the hunters themselves. One local farmer-hunter felt a twig tickle the back of his neck. Looking up, he discovered the freshly cut stub of a small branch nearly a foot above him. The whole group suddenly felt a little shaky in the knees.

In the meantime, Scrub's knees were serving him very well. He plunged on at full speed for nearly a mile, then dropped into a thicket and again lay still.

Chapter 18:
One Boy, One Arrow

As Scrub lay quietly resting, the afternoon sky turned gray and the air became chilled. The buck was not uncomfortable from the cold, but he felt the approach of a storm. Instinct told him to find a more protected spot, with plenty of evergreens for both shelter and food.

Two miles to the west, a spring-fed stream flowed out of a small cedar swamp. It was as far from human dwellings or roads as a deer could get in that general area. By mid-afternoon snow began to fall-lightly at first, but steadily increasing. Winter was coming early. Scrub rose, shook himself, and headed west - into the wind.

Back in their cabin, the hunters built a warm fire, pulled off their boots, and relaxed. After a big dinner they looked out at the gathering storm and relaxed some more - all but one, that is.

The boy who had flushed Scrub from behind his log could not forget that "rack of horns". He had seen those ten points sailing over the bushes as Scrub sailed away. Blurred against a background of brush, those points had seemed like many more than ten - at least 20 or 30 he had boasted. The laughter that greeted his claim only made him the more determined to prove it.

Now, as he looked out at the falling snow, a plan grew in his mind. He had been born in this very cabin. He knew every inch of the woods for miles around. Scrub was no stranger to him. Every time he had seen the Big Buck those points had increased in size and number, aided by a lively imagination.

The boy's prize possession was a fiberglass, 30 pound bow and a half dozen steel-tipped hunting arrows. The men, engrossed in tall tales of mighty bucks and even mightier hunters, did not notice the boy slip out into the storm.

In his mind the nature-wise young hunter pictured Scrub heading west toward the protection of the cedar swamp. It was the natural place for a deer to go. The boy headed north. In ten minutes he had found Scrub's track leading west. It could not be very old. There was only a little snow in the track itself. The wind was in the boy's favor. It would carry both sound and scent behind him - away from the Big Buck.

The afternoon was far gone. The boy must hurry if he was going to collect the 20 point rack he had boasted about. For half a mile the boy ran. Then the tracks became so fresh that he slowed to a careful stalk. There were signs that the buck was stopping to browse here and there. Suddenly the young hunter remembered. There was a wild apple tree in a small clearing just ahead. He stepped more cautiously. The Big Buck just had to be there.

As the boy neared the clearing, the woods began to thin out. A hedge of sumac ringed the opening. The young hunter crouched low, using the sumac as a screen. Now he had reached the last large tree. He hugged up to it and peered cautiously around it. There he was - the Big Buck - head down calmly eating an apple he had pawed from the snow. The rack seemed bigger than ever. The boy began to count -3-4-5-8-9 he must have made a mistake. There had to be more than ten!

Scrub raised his head. A quick glance around and then one more apple. As Scrub lowered his head again the boy moved from behind the tree and stepped forward - bow and arrow ready. Then he froze. The buck's head was up. Nothing moving, more apple, head down again. The bow string twanged. Scrub's head jerked up. A feathered shaft drove half its length into the Big Buck's side. His white tail flashed and he was gone. The boy shook all over - he felt weak in the knees from "buck fever". But he knew he had scored a solid hit. He wanted to run after the deer, but he remembered what his father had told him - "Wait five minutes. Let the deer stop and bleed."

During those next few minutes night seemed to settle down suddenly. Dark clouds rolled overhead. The wind howled and drove blinding snow across the clearing. With a start the young hunter realized there would be no tracks to follow. He rushed to the apple tree, barely visible now in the clearing. There was the spot where Scrub had pawed for apples, but beyond that the wind had wiped out all tracks. The boy knew a good hunter should follow up on his shot. But the sudden squall had left nothing to follow. He could scarcely tell which way was home. An old logging road led out of the clearing through the woods and back near his cabin. He stumbled into it and headed for home.

The boy's excitement gave way to a strange loneliness. He was sure he would never again meet the Big Buck he had come to admire during the past three years. Scrub ran with a desperation he had not known since his first summer when the dogs had nearly ended his life. It seemed that his strength was flowing out through the wound in his side. His legs felt wobbly as they had been during the hard winter when starvation threatened. When had he felt so tired? He would not go on - why should he? Nothing followed. There was no gunfire - no howling dogs - nothing. He slowed to a walk. Carefully he picked his way into a cedar thicket. He lay down on his good side. He was so tired, and the snow felt so restful.

Morning dawned, bright and clear. Still Scrub rested under his cedar thicket. A yellow-feathered shaft thrust up through a mound of snow. Two of his ten points stuck like a dead forked stick. They would never hang in a sportsman's trophy room. A hungry coyote threaded the brush nearby. His gray nose sniffed the air, then howled an invitation to his mate. But Scrub did not stir in his shroud of white.